SQUARE DANCING
at
THE ASYLUM

Nouveau Noir Flash Fiction

Kirby Wright

ISBN: 0974106771
ISBN-13: 978-0974106779

Published by Lemon Shark Press
San Diego, California
www.lemonsharkpress.com
ISBN: 0974106771
ISBN-13: 978-0974106779
Copyright © 2013 by Kirby Wright
All Rights Reserved

LEMON SHARK
PRESS

In memory of my great uncle Paul Ford Nolan

Lifelong patient at Worcester State Hospital,

Worcester, MA

SQUARE DANCING AT THE ASYLUM

ACKNOWLEDGEMENTS

The author wishes to thank the editors and staff of the following publications in which some of these works first appeared or are forthcoming: *Arabesques Review, Ascent Aspirations Magazine, B: an Anthology of Barbie Poems, Bayou Magazine, Black Heart Magazine, Blinking Cursor, Blue Mesa Review, Calliope, The Coachella Review, Concho River Review, The Conium Review, Connotation Press, The Fiddleback, Flash: The International Short-Short Story Magazine, Floorboard Review, The Foliate Oak Literary Magazine, Front Range Review, FutureCycle Press, Gambling the Aisle, Gargoyle, Gravel Magazine, Great Weather for Media, Hawai'i Review, Hayden's Ferry Review, In Posse Review, Line Zero, The Literary Bohemian, Mad Hattters' Review, Marco Polo Arts Magazine, Meat for Tea: The Valley Review, The Medulla Review, The Monarch Review, Monkey Puzzle, Moonshot Magazine, Neon Literary Magazine, Owen Wister Review, Paris Lit Up, Pif Magazine, Pithead Chapel, Poetry Quarterly, The Portland Review, Prime Mincer, Printer's Devil Review, The Quotable, Red Earth Review, Red Ochre Press, San Pedro River Review, The Prose-Poem Project, The Santa Clara Review, Santa Fe Literary Review, Seems, Sein und Werden, Sentence, Shadowbox, Shenandoah, SLAB, Slipstream, Temenos, Tipton Poetry Journal, Toyon, Tributaries, Washington Square, Wilderness House Literary Review, Writer's Bloc, Zouch Magazine,* and *Zymbol.*

CONTENTS

FOREWORD

Book 1: DESIRE

Book 2: THE BURBS

Book 3: CONFINEMENT

Book 4: CREATURE COMFORTS

Book 5: SLAUGHTERHOUSE FLIES

Book 6: NOTES FROM THE FRONT LINE

Book 7: NOTHING EVER CHANGES

FOREWORD

I don't always know from watching what is gymnastics and what is dance. Listening doesn't always tell me which tunes are country and which are rock or even pop. All the same, as sure as *Gymnopedies* is ballet, I know what is beautiful. I know what reaches me, and what changes me. *Square Dancing at the Asylum* is beautiful even when it turns angular and confrontative. It reaches me like fog through open windows, inescapably. And I don't even try to resist the change in myself Wright effects with these bolts of flashing literature.

Why would I expose myself to art if I were going to reject its constructive power?

Kirby Wright calls his pieces "flash fiction." Would any reader feel differently about them if he called them poems, prose poetry, or just very short stories? I think serious readers would not. The pieces are poetry because they are aesthetically whole and they depend on all the significant qualities of language, not just the defined meanings of the words. They are very short stories, since that only means each one can be read in basically no time. Are they prose poetry or flash fiction?

Easy question. Yes!

What is far less easy is to keep yourself from being entirely consumed by the seven "books" in the volume. Even the names of the books recited in order suggest something more than the naming of "sections" in a collection: Desire, The Burbs, Confinement, Creature Comforts, Slaughterhouse Flies, Notes From the Front Line, and Nothing Ever Changes.

The major characters—all gunning for you—include a lifelong mental patient, cannibals, an abusive father, a narcissist mother, a possessive big brother, and a helpless kid sister. There are countless other characters that will haunt and taunt you ever after too, including one who will make you think twice about any poems you ever try to write yourself: "The Queen of Above Average Poetry."

Prose poems have been around for at least 150 years. Oscar Wilde was a master of the form. Flash fiction, more than anything, seems to be a newish (1990 or so) name for the same form, probably meant to place fewer demands on the writer about the intense, poetic use of those higher and more subtle qualities of language. Wright didn't need the softer definition. Throughout *Square Dancing,* there is rhythm and multiplication of possible meaning, words provide color, and sounds convey emotions. Nonetheless, Wright is smart enough to use the newer name for his work: flash fiction.

It is not possible to know and probably not reasonable to guess what a writer "thinks he is doing," ever. We cannot see what he is looking at, know what he is thinking, or sense the feelings that move the creator of art in any form, especially literature. We can, however, be moved by his language. Here's an example: in "Earthquake Weather" you'll read, "humming Iran's National Anthem at intersections." That plugs into my heartbeat, and gives it a new rhythm. Even completely out of context, the syllables stun. Or, try this one from "New Jersey" as both an intense use of language and an ultra-sharp image: "Neighbors laugh, cough, conduct seizures of sneezes during family reunions."

There are, all through *Square Dancing at the Asylum*, endings that surprise (or even shock) the reader, but they never feel contrived. Before you even read the book—I know you'll want to read it—try to think how this ending of "Hurricane Irene" is a direction-changing surprise: "The breeze makes him feel he as though he's really there. He sees a woman standing at the water's edge, searching for something in the waves."

Heart-stoppers can crop up anywhere in this collection. You won't understand why this is so important until you read your way to it, but burn this "Messages From the West" line into memory: "After crossing the Golden Gate Bridge, the man adjusts his rearview mirror while speeding home to Michigan, his convertible top down."

Whole novels blossom in your thoughts or dreams after you read a few hundred words. The pieces do not appear as Cliff notes. Instead, each piece is clearly the crystallized result of powerfully and passionately compressing every meaningful thought and syllable into almost no space, giving meaning so concentrated it is dizzying.

There are echoes throughout *Square Dancing at the Asylum* to remind you of Wright's memoirs, his earlier poetry, and even his speculative fiction (*The End, My Friend*). You don't have to be familiar with these earlier works to enjoy the new volume, but this is a collection that—if it is your introduction to Wright—will send you in search of his other works. First, though, stop and enjoy the prose here, or the poems, or flash fictions. Doesn't matter. Turn the pages slowly. Give yourself time to think and care about what you're experiencing as you read. The meaning and value will grow to fill all the time you are willing to give them.

—Joseph W. Bean, Book Critic, MAUI WEEKLY

BOOK 1

DESIRE

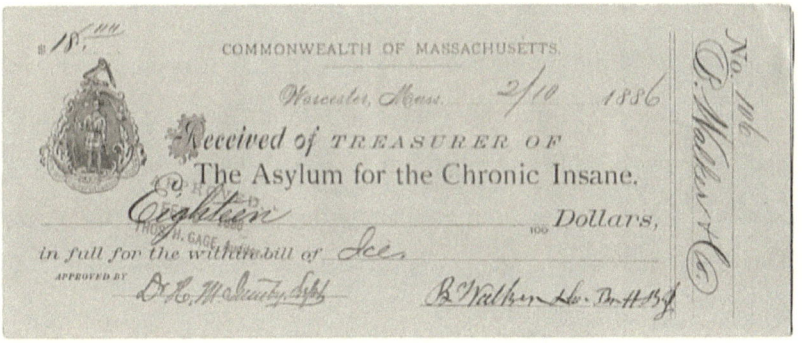

BAIT

THE FIRE DIES. I throw in a chair with lion-headed arms for warmth. Paws extend back into my bedroom, claws scratching stone.

My room has sliding a glass door. Students slide it open, stroll past my bed, and leave through an oak door. I am the campus shortcut. A coed wearing a mini and platinum bouffant enters. She locks the glass and takes off her bouffant. She's bald. "I'm Bait," she goes, unbuckling her skirt. She tears off strips that were eyebrows. "Velcro," she admits.

We listen to the chair howl. Bait moves against me—I want to resist, yet can't. I feel as if I'm cheating on a lover. "Eat," she instructs. "Eat like a shark." Bait forces me to do things I ordinarily would not do. Soon I learn the taste of her salt.

MONA

MONA TAKES A MORPHINE shot. A pharmacist has administered it at our house, after sterilizing her arm with a wet cotton ball. "Wow," I say, "a house call." I want morphine too, but I'm afraid of needles. Mona lies on the bed, drops her head on the pillow. She smiles. The pharmacist leaves. "Good?" I ask. "So good," Mona says, closing her eyes. She falls asleep smiling. She looks like a sleeping Mona Lisa

I leave the house. I'm on a bicycle in the rain. Not a heavy rain, a drizzle. I'm on my way to CVS to track down the pharmacist. If find the pharmacy but it's a different pharmacist. This one wants to administer penicillin, not morphine. I'm in a room sitting on a steel table. The pharmacist rolls up my sleeve over my shoulder. He has syringe and cotton ball. "No," I say.

I run out and mount the bicycle. My bike is small. The tires are off-road, the knobby kind. I pedal fast approaching a curb. It's raining now, not drizzling. I must get home to Mona. I'm on Middlefield Road in Palo Alto. I try a wheelie over the curb but forget to tug on the handlebars. The impact hurts. A weather report blares from an invisible radio:

THIS IS A SURPRISE STORM. BEWARE.

BIGGEST STORM OF THE YEAR. LAST

REAL RAIN BEFORE SUMMER. SMALL

CRAFT ADVISORIES IN EFFECT FOR ALL

COASTAL WATERS. ACCIDENTS ON EVERY

BRIDGE. BIGGEST STORM EVER.

I pedal fast. I feel like a hamster on a wheel, grinding away at the gears. When I get home, she has her head on the pillow. She is a sedated Mona Lisa. Her skin? Oils. She is a picture, a framed replacement. "Where's the real Mona?" I ask, shaking the picture. No answer. I shake again. Still no reply. I'm mad at myself for leaving and for not taking the morphine. "Chicken," I mutter. I hang her up on the bedroom wall—she seems sad, more melancholy than I remember.

BELL'S PALSY FOR TWO

MY BEST FRIEND Rich returns from the dead for our high school reunion. He killed himself last year for being gay. Rich's hanging out at the punch bowl wearing a 2-button seersucker suit and a cobalt tie with a black diamond pattern. I feel foolish in jeans. He's got Bell's palsy like me but his case doesn't look as serious. I ask if he can smile. "Just a little," he replies, lifting the left side of his mouth. His teeth flash. Funny, my palsy affects the opposite side. I compliment Rich on his duds. "It's what Mom buried me in," he mutters, dipping a ladle into the punch. "Are you still with Mandy?" he asks. I tell him yes, that I love her and that now she's my fiancée. He fumbles his glass, spilling punch on his suit. I ask if something's wrong. Rich gives a half-smile.

PSYCHE IN LINGERIE

WE FIND a pink mountain. The mineral glitters in her hand. "What is it?" Psyche asks. "Bauxite," I reply. Spots are soft, unstable, sucking like quicksand. We hike until we reach a waterfall. We walk over water, stepping on stone islands. Statues surround us. One's half-fish and half-man: a man's head on a neck of gills. The legs are fins but the arms human. Fishman. Psyche rubs against a statue of Eros, cooling in the breeze from the falling water. "Careful," I warn. She smiles and goes, "Paranoid." Something moves and I turn— Fishman's wiggling. "He's alive!" I say. He wiggles free of his pedestal and swims through the air to reach Psyche. She bends to stroke. Fishman wags his tail. She straddles his back. "No!" I call. Psyche grabs his dorsal fin and he dives her into the bauxite. She's gone. The waterfall stops. The statues melt. The mountain flattens into a desert. The sky turns violet. I find a mirror on a rock and brush off the bauxite. I look in—Psyche's wearing red lingerie on our bed and fingering snapshots. Fishman swims over and opens his mouth. His gills flare as he swallows our lives, one memory at a time.

AT THE COFFEE HOUSE

SHE STANDS beside the doorway watching him wait in line with his old college buddy. "Tall Americano," he orders. He wears the aqua shorts she picked out to show off his buns, and a dobby hat to hide the salt in his hair. There are girls behind him, coeds really, and he starts flirting. A blonde with hair past her waist giggles at something he says. The old college buddy joins in and it becomes a party. So many smiles, so much flashing of teeth.

She steps back into twilight. She doesn't want coffee or cheesecake. It's something they do as a couple, but the old college buddy makes her feel like a third wheel. She sits at a brick fire pit on the patio. The flames are orange and green. She spots him through glass—he clutches a venti-sized cup and performs exaggerated gestures like a silent movie star. The blonde is smiling. She hears the old college buddy's machinegun laugh. She kicks off her slippers. She swings bare feet up on brick, toes reaching for fire.

PUMPKIN PATCH

ON THE OVERPASS, we drive above fields of yellow grass. We saw an accident. "That's Pumpkin Patch," she says, pointing down. Below, a clearing. We take the next exit and backtrack. The air is hot. Humid. Men holding sickles signal us off the asphalt. We follow a dirt road through the grass. A black Cadillac follows. We reach a street of abandoned homes.

"Like when I was a kid," she says.

"What?" I ask.

She licks her lips. "Trick-or-Treat."

The homes are in good shape. Picture windows overlook the street. We park and walk past one home that isn't preserved—pink paint peeling, rotting wood, rusty wrought iron gratings. The Caddy cruises by with the passenger taking photographs.

"People still live here," she says.

"Trick-or-Treat?"

I want to knock to prove her wrong. It's a ghost town. A carved pumpkin sits at a window inside one of the homes. Funny, I hadn't noticed that before. I look up and down the street: now every window has a pumpkin.

"Our house awaits," she says.

"Which one?" I ask.

"The one without a pumpkin."

"We have to move in?"

"Sure do," she says, "remember, we had that accident."

THE PINK BALLOON

THE PINK BALLOON flies above the fair, a dream lost in the sky. The jet stream hurls it into the clouds. A boy on an Airbus sees pink just beyond the steel wing of his plane. The helium inside weakens. A downdraft catches the balloon. It falls into a crater and lands on a secret lake. A pelican snaps at it, thinking it's a puffy salmon. "I am not edible!" the balloon tells the pelican, but they don't speak the same language. The balloon drifts into the bird's belly. It remembers the girl who picked it out from over 100 balloons, holding it tight by the tail.

FLORIDIAN DREAMS OF LUST AND REGRET

REAL ESTATE flags fly the perimeter of Jellystone Retirement. Welcome to detached homes, hurricanes, Futurestone driveways. Sun spills through the window, paints my corn flakes yellow.

Wife and I went different directions under the same roof. She stayed home to baby her housebound syndrome. I slept off oysters back at the office. I remember vacationing on twin beds. After a seven-year drought, I genuflect at our old waterbed, pray for sex in Heaven.

Ever do a mannequin? Greek statue? Blowup doll? Now is as true as oranges. Morning hands the ball off to afternoon. Afternoon runs interference. The Matterhorn glows in the distance. Squirrels scale the roof and slip on my oily shingles. A jet moves as if pulled by a string, silver echoing gun.

Wife wears costumes—mascara, blonde wig, black dress—anything for young. I exercise my heart with extra-large coffee. Minutes tangle up in hours. Freedom means fleeing the mall and speeding out of Catholic parking lots.

In retirement, participants grow. The sun burns cold pleasure, poaches optimism out of the groves. Passing trains play the harmonica. The phone rings once, twice. Wife consoles our twice-divorced daughter. Bulldozers cook raw earth beyond the asphalt.

Bikini girls stroll the flat screen. I rub old trophies, remember kissing

11

under the bleachers. These days, everything stings.

Never throw a turtle into a chlorinated pool. I once saw a seagull with green feathers perched on a fountain. I live in nightmares imagining, projecting alohas on flat horizons.

Gays play it straight at the community theater, flaunt closet dramas at the senile audience. A bald man guzzles Jack Daniels from one-shot bottles. The curtain closes. Bravo, bravo, excellent performances! Backstage girls chase one another with rolled-up towels.

After exits and bottles, wrinkled bodies patch up holes.

BELL'S PALSY

BELL'S PALSY HIT, paralyzing the right side of Dick's visage. An eye refused to close. He couldn't whistle. Half his facial wrinkles melted away. Neighbors thought he'd either gotten a cheap facelift or was experiencing botched Botox. Others were convinced he'd had a stroke since he could only speak out of the left side of his mouth. His cornea deteriorated. Dick was forced to wear an eye patch and children figured he was a pirate. He took a cue from them and, on Halloween, he dressed as Blackbeard. "Yo, ho, ho," he'd chant handing out candy, a stuffed parrot perched on his shoulder.

Dick got sick of the eye that wouldn't close. He had a surgeon slice open his lid and sew in a sliver of gold. The gold challenged the muscles and now he struggled to keep the eye open. Still, he felt it was a good thing. *Like lifting weights*, he thought. No longer did he need to tape the lid shut at night. Soon his dreams were dominated by gold prospecting in exotic locales, such as Prague and Hong Kong. His dream girl was half-Czech and half-Chinese. She smacked Dick with shots of espresso so he'd keep hunting gold and couldn't escape by waking. His lid twitched hysterically in bed as his pick struck the mother lode in Cairo.

EARTHQUAKE WEATHER

WE LUNCH in Country Club sun. Fiancée's dialogue mimics her tan, anorexic Aunt. Aunt leans forward, never burns. Golfers chase balls, distill in heat. My neck muscles lobster pasta. Aunt pink lips a mint julep. Planes dip wings and swim like beetles across a blue pond. Earthquake weather.

Dentist Dan says I'm grinding in nightmares. Patients refuse elevators up to his 3rd floor, complain about plate tectonics, getting stuck. Dan says I've got teeth of a man two decades older. I chew my teeth like gum, in private, grinding fear into dentin. Blonde assistant pulls vest over my head, the latest in designer lead. Dan uses a 3-D chart to discuss holes and fillings. It's assembly. Numbing routine. Novocain lines. During root canal, Dan dreams Venice, gondolas, goblets of scarlet wine.

I'm famous for self-delusion, deluding lovers, eating asphalt on corners, humming Iran's National Anthem at intersections. Horizon spreads smog through clandestine sky. Fiancée learns the limbo, climbs a pole to test the strength of a Chinatown street lamp. Panties flap like flags outside a rooming house window.

The moon is the most overrated tool—it measures Aunt as new nation. Sun skateboards west. Lawnmowers celebrate weekends with

30-weight oil. Drink weeds off Freeway 280 as you drift synthetic ocean. Tires blow inland, filled with conquered wind. Does air shrink with age? Hawks swoop, powered by dove hunger. Desire for conquest shifts the soul. Dadio fell in love with his Volvo. Relationships all over the world get surrounded by wood, either living or dead, go unfinished or finished.

Shadows fall on a motel wall. Fiancée phones long distance. Aunt bends in the Aloha Inn. The mattress trembles—8 on the Richter scale. Tan lines wrinkle. A sparrow flits east, toward the ballpoint eye of my pen.

PURPLE SUMMER

EXAMINE MY HAIR: you'll discover black strands tinged purple. I buy cheap products at CVS, in boxes picturing macho men.

Today I hunch on a park bench holding a bag of peanuts. Girls in skirts stroll a walkway that circles the park. One rides a bike. I love watching their calves flex and the way they sweep hair out of their faces whenever it breezes. A mangy squirrel stands on its haunches. If I ever got lucky with one of the skirts, I doubt it would last past sunset. I mean, my cock limps like a plucked violet. Ankles ache with arthritis. Right eye frozen by Bell's palsy. Still, after applying the dye, I feel a decade younger.

A blonde rollerblades over and flops on my bench. I love how the slats shift beneath me accepting her weight. She chews gum while tying her lace. Her white skirt hikes up over her thighs. She is my Aphrodite. I extend a peanut to the mangy squirrel—he snatches it and scampers away.

"Cute," goes Aphrodite.

"I could be arrested," I whisper.

"Why?"

"Illegal to feed 'em."

Aphrodite blows a bubble and pops it. "I like rebels," she chews, "especially men who help small animals."

Her teeth are teenage white, the color of promise and unbridled passion. I scoot closer, until I'm an arm length away. Aphrodite smells like watermelon. I touch her wrist. My cock flinches. My fingers move through the white blonde hairs on her forearm up to a beauty mark below her spaghetti-strapped shoulder. She leans, until her blonde hair rests against my chest and rollerblades dangle off the edge of the bench.

"You're nice," she coos. "How old are you anyway?"

"The age of a young college professor."

"35?"

"A wee bit more," I reply, touching her hair. It feels like silk.

"Are you older than, my father?"

"How old is the dear man?"

"45."

I gaze across the grass. The sun balances the horizon like a tightrope artist walking a rope. Will there be a green flash? The mangy squirrel watches me from the crotch of a pine. Aphrodite takes her head off my chest. She taps a blade on the cement below and studies my face. I'm glad my frozen eye's hidden behind sunglasses and that she can't see my crow's feet. My ankle aches.

Aphrodite runs a hand through my scalp, studying my hair. "Sick," she blurts, "you're purple."

"Yes," I nod. "I use store-bought products."

"Ew," she goes, rubbing her arm. "Why'd you fuckin' touch me?"

The slats flex as she jerks up off the bench. "Perv," she hisses, grabbing the bench for support. I watch her skate off, blades grinding cement like a meat cutter's saw moving through bone. Aphrodite races west into the half-drowned sun, a silhouette dancing a purple canvas.

PRINCESS CATHY IN THE LAND OF REGRET

FACE IT, CATHY, you're a scanned copy of your father. You want to be in control like him. Watch Daddy frown and cross his arms in family movies. See Mummy (once a Swedish beauty queen) turn invisible when Daddy scolds. You practiced his technique on yourself by refusing to eat in high school. But you didn't want to get too thin because you might vanish. You always knew your ideal man would be weak, although touched by a certain magic (that magic requirement coincided with young Daddy's mate hunt too—that's why he picked a beauty queen from Gotland resembling Cinderella).

You find a short, stocky hippie singing in a northern bar—his brogue lilt melts your icy heart. He reminds you of one of the Seven Dwarfs, only a Scottish version. You imagine him sprinkled with fairy dust and realize he's fated to be your Prince when he sings your requested "Edelweiss." You marry, make babies on a bearskin rug, and live in the snowy north until the children grow up and head south. Now you're alone with the Prince. He has a home office so you bump into him all the time. You laugh during these bumps, but it gets annoying. Sometimes he flies off to Scotland to play gigs. When he returns, you feel lonelier than when he was gone. You realize your life partner is a minstrel version of Bashful. You feel strange. Maybe you never really loved this hippie and only married him for his ability to disappear whenever you crossed your arms and tapped your shoe on the floor.

I like your new hobby. Your fingers jab laptop keys as you quest for lost loves in cyber space. Are they still alive? Are they still where you left them? Your blood feels young as desires surface. The desires fuse with once-dormant feelings you consider evil, things like Envy, Bitterness, and Hate. The desires and feelings become strands of rope that intertwine, a weaving that forms a gray quilt splashed with pink, red, and green. The quilt unfurls, covering acres inside you. "Welcome to the Land of Regret," you moan. You're tempted to shut the laptop. But you don't. You flash to John Woodrow, the thin guy you met in the Munich hospital. He had a dry wit and joked about catching hepatitis eating shellfish in Budapest. "Cath," pleads a brogue voice, "come to bed." You Google but can't find John, only teens and a fat man sharing his name. You recall a singsong voice and decide he was gay. You dig out albums from high school and college. Whatever happened to Brian McCullough, your hunky date at the Senior Prom? You find Brian selling cars in Tulsa. He owns a Kia dealership and his cartoon likeness floats on a sign above the showroom. "The Brian that got away," you lament. Then you hunt for "Mr. Right," the model-cute collegiate you let tongue your breasts after he treated you to moo shu pork at Double Happiness, the one who left in a huff when you refused to go all the way. You can't imagine Mr. Right ever walking down the aisle. If he did, he couldn't have married a beauty because you knew he was using his own good looks (Prince Charming handsome) as a trump card for control. Loving him was verboten. After all, you were Daddy. You were the controller. You Google two more loves, acquaintances really, until the hippie pleads again. You pray his next UK trip comes quick. "Dream time," you surrender, collapsing the screen and sliding your laptop under the bearskin rug.

BOOK 2

THE BURBS

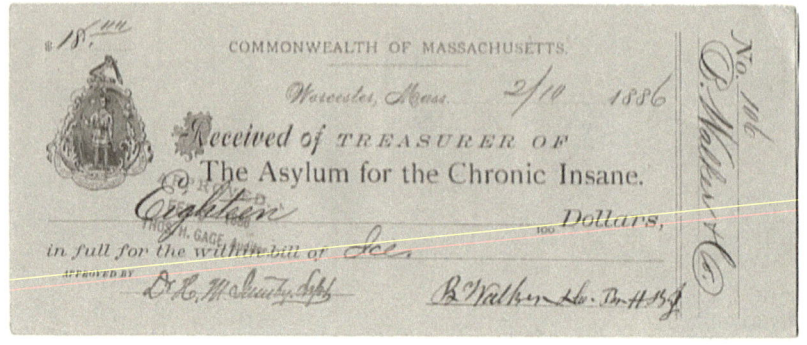

SUMMER TOWN

MY STREET? Strip of yellow lawns, oil-stained driveways, For Sale signs. A girl without eyes stares out the neighboring window. Asphalt shatters the cul-de-sac. Women push strollers past a popped beach ball skinning the gutter blue.

I'm knotted in apron frosting a cake. The room for entertaining fills with strangers. Most seem older. I recall photo albums stacked in the garage beside the bag of charcoal. When I was young I was way above average. Grandfather toasts—wine glasses rise. Who are these people? Outside, sun scorches the drive.

CAT

I SWEAR, my cat's on speed. Either that or bath salts. She delights in staying up all night to bug me. She starts by slipping her head through the slats in the blinds and moaning. Then she sharpens her claws on the carpet before leaping on the shelf to moonwalk the tops of books. "Stop that!" I always say. She reaches up and knocks down pictures of my fiancée. One of the frames is shattered. I can't figure her out. Is it my new cat food that's made by that has-been actor? Who knows. I should toss her outside, let her strut the twilight among strange cats until the moon dies.

NEIGHBORS

IS THAT the message machine talking? No. It's my ex yelling at her boyfriend in their house on the hill. "Goddamn you," she goes, "you horrible man!" She likes him because he takes it the way her mother took it from her father all those years ago in Newport. The boyfriend can't escape because he's on disability and doesn't own a car. Sometimes he wheelchairs into their backyard, throws tangerines that roll to my patio. Yesterday one hit the roof. I'd toss them back but that would start a war. "Where the hell are you?" my ex calls.

BALD

THAT BALD GUY on the hill is yelling at his dog again. For what, I don't know. Sometimes I hear him yelling at his wife and kids. Once he yelled at a sparrow. He's not a natural bald. On the contrary, I'm certain he shaves his crown at least twice a week because I've seen a 5 O'clock shadow when he patrols our fence. The shadow makes him look like a convict. I'll bet he'd go for the convict look if they'd let him get away with it at work. Being bald probably makes him feel tough. But he's not tough. He has a cream puff belly and spindly arms like Tyrannosaurus Rex. I doubt he could fight his way out of a paper bag. He was barbecuing one Sunday when his wife joined him at the Weber Kettle—she cussed him, and then lifted her leg like a dog. That's the only time I ever heard him laugh.

BONE ON BONE

WELL HELLO, Mary, this is June. It's been ages since we last talked. Would you like to go to lunch some time next week? Oh. I didn't know that about Harold. Where is the cancer? Oh, my. My goodness. That darn cancer. Cancer of the liver. There's really nothing they can do for him? Imagine that, cancer of the liver. I'm so sorry. Now how has Barbara been feeling? Oh? You should send her to Doctor Kane. He does most of the hips and the knees. When I had my hip replaced, I prayed so hard, and God really came through for me. Dr. Kane did the operation and what a relief. My hip's made of that real strong stuff, I think they call it tit, tit-tan. Yes, that's it. Tit-tanium. Every time he took an X-ray he couldn't believe it, bone on bone. One bone rubbing against another. I had one of the worst cases, and I know it was because of the steroids. Those darn steroids go straight for the cartilage. Do one thing to help something and it destroys something else. Really? Did you take one every day? So, the spots are gone? That's wonderful. Now tell me about your new neighbor's at Lola's old house. Really. I don't even know our next-door neighbors. Two doctors, a man and a woman with a little child. They're Oriental. The whole block's turned Oriental. See how things change? Are you sure you wouldn't be able to go to lunch some day? Oh, that's okay. Well, do give my best to Barbara. Harold will be in my prayers. Yes. Good-bye.

ADVICE FOR PREPARING A HUSBAND

LUG HONEYBUNCH into the bathroom and plop him on the toilet, arms and legs akimbo. Use a straight edge to shave cheeks, jaw line, and neck. Leave the sideburns. And don't touch those hairs sprouting out of his third eye. Trim eyebrows and nails. Now into the tub. Shower him in hot water and begin to soap. That's it, really work that lather into armpits, groin, and anus. Smells better already, right? Finish with a lukewarm wash, pat dry, then drag into your bedroom and flop him on the mattress. Pull on boxers and navy blue socks. I suggest the seersucker or camel hair blazer with the cream shirt, white linen trousers, and emerald tie. What? You already promised the camel hair to Harry two doors down? No way. Then go with the seersucker but keep everything else status quo, and don't forget the faux ivory cufflinks. It's cool to dab on aftershave but no splashing. Wow, he seems alive lying there, as if resting before Mass. I agree, he does look shorter than in real life. Excellent work. Hubby's A+ ready for planting at high noon.

GARAGE SALE

MOVING ALREADY? Wow. Sorry to see you go. Does that DVD player still work? Five free movies will sweeten the deal. You know, we moved to Portico the same year you guys did. Ten years ago? Time sure flies. Now that I think about it, I could really use that fondue set next to the stationary walker. Hey, let's pretend we've been good friends while I dig through boxes of cookbooks, baby books and paperbacks, looking for god knows what. That blonde Ikea looks brand new. I promise not to bring up the SEC thing and your insider trading scandal. Oh! I love the his-and-her black leather jackets hanging off the tree. I know this sounds odd, but one summer I was sure you kept your adopted daughter a prisoner in her room on the second floor, after I spotted little girl hands crawling the glass. Call me crazy. I can't believe you're selling Victoria's Secret. Moving van same day as the trash? Well, have a great new life in New Mexico. You guys deserve it.

POETIC LICENSE

EVERYONE HAS a book out these days, including my cat. She paws couplets about being mistreated, not getting three squares, and being put on a diet. Another big gripe is getting cooped up all day in the apartment while I'm at work. What can I do? She should realize someone needs to bring home the bacon on wet days when the world is mute and the only sounds are wind and rain on the roof.

SELLER'S MARKET

THE NEIGHBORS are selling their house. The sign out front says POOL in red letters. "15 offers so far," smiles the Realtor. Sometimes I see her watering the lawn. Occasionally I see him walking the dog. We'd exchange waves before they grew reclusive after he got his name in the paper for insider trading. Their son just started college. Their daughter won a ribbon for riding a horse. They're moving out to a ranch in the desert. "Closer to work," goes the Realtor. Doubt I'll ever see them again.

FATHER'S DAY

THE SIDE IS FALLING off something next-door. You can hear the wife scream it. The husband continues to barbecue. He thinks of her as a pesky roommate, someone who's mediocre at casseroles yet spreads her legs after a bottle of wine. He wonders what will happen after they polish off the syrah, when it's just the two of them camped on the deck overlooking a hill of weeds. Now she's screaming about smoke in the house. He flips the burgers, smiling.

THE TRAIN FROM CHICAGO

I STAND between my mother and Dadio on the loading platform at Union Station in Los Angeles. My grandfather's train from Chicago is coming. My mother calls him "Popsy." His nickname for her is "June Spoon." I am seven and have never met him.

"Why didn't Popsy fly?" I ask.

June Spoon puts her hand on my head. "He's too scared to fly."

"I'm not scared."

"Then that can mean only one thing, Kirbo," says Dadio.

"What?"

"You're braver."

June Spoon told me Popsy lives in a small apartment on the ninth floor of the Pick-Congress Hotel. He promised to pay for her wedding but things didn't work out. "Piker," Dadio said when I asked about it.

I remember the black and white—Popsy wears a suit, tie, and tilted hat. The hat casts a shadow, cutting his face in half. Sparky the

Parakeet sits on his shoulder. Popsy doesn't smile. I feel, if he didn't have Sparky, he'd have no one. I doubt there's anybody who cares whether his feet are warm at night or if there's food in his fridge.

Popsy rarely phones. When he does, he doesn't ask to speak to me. I know long distance is expensive. Sometimes June Spoon sends secret money and there is always a few hundred on Christmases and birthdays. He said the money saves him when he gets behind. He rarely saw her after Gert caught him with a woman in a Boston bar a week after June Spoon's tenth birthday.

He sends me cards but no gifts. Once he surprised Troy with a toy submarine. Troy played with it in the tub until it rusted away. June Spoon told me Popsy was a stockbroker during the Roaring Twenties and paid cash for a new Cole 8 sedan every year. He bought a red piano for the party room he'd built in their Waltham basement. Gert played the piano while June Spoon tapped and sang Broadway show tunes.

"You'll be a big star someday," Popsy said, clapping wildly after her final note.

"Big as Shirley Temple, Popsy?"

"Bigger, June Spoon. Much, much bigger."

NEW JERSEY

COUPLES EMBRACE in the community ballroom. Girls not asked to dance giggle confessionals; the one as tall as a palm winks at the married mailman.

Haul in the coal. Burn it. Swing in the backyard hammock. Telephone poles crucify intentions. Fireflies fat, full of light, becoming flying flashlights to ignite grandparents' faces. I sweat pearls of beer under a giant clay priest pointing west from a knoll above the expressway.

Neighbors laugh, cough, conduct seizures of sneezes during family reunions. Most arrest memories raking leaves and pouring circular driveways. Weekend bedrooms distill the silence. Fall asleep during commercials? We are our own best tortures.

Children play patterns, claim victories and defeats on asphalt. Sun moans toward eclipse under the fences. Trees gleam various greens. Wind is generous, samples the wax on parked cars. Garage sales introduce neighbors to easy museums. A minute is a dot on a second-hand clock. The sun calls the long day, turns the ball over to twilight. Suburbs are powered by weekend promises. Girls bathe tonsils in street corner beer, tan themselves orange under halogens.

A brown bag rolls like a tumbleweed across the pavement. Boy becomes his father behind the wheel: he fears cul-de-sac traffic through a rearview mirror covered with webs. Wind whispers whiskey and soda. A dove bears down on a Styrofoam cup, swallows greedy, morphs into an industrial bird of prey.

Who inherits the metal? A neighbor watching college football fingers his sandwich made hours earlier from dolphin-safe tuna. He bites into mercury. A jagged spear of light hurls into an alarm clock bolted to his living room wall. Downtown, his wife enjoys her mani-pedi.

A divorcee jogs her platinum hair on long waxy legs. Fathers and sons allow her to enter their souls. She splits nuclear families apart spitting store-bought light. Clouds hemorrhage orange.

Cars display dents. Planes the intensity of Venus pretend to be 100-watt lights. Roofs are hats covering the bald spots of owners. Wind acts as a cushion for ghosts. Hear sirens? The Earth could crack under the ambulance fog, spilling forth ancestors. I consider debris and am happy for routine decay, suburban ennui, things fermenting in humidity.

BOOK 3

CONFINEMENT

SQUARE DANCING AT THE ASYLUM

MY FAMILY'S VERY disappointed in me. They've been disappointed for years. The last straw was when Mother caught me with my hand in the store register and then with my fingers in Virginia's panties. Virginia's my redheaded sister. A week later I was riding the rails west. I lived on pork and beans and carried underwear, a bar of soap, and a toothbrush in my knapsack. I liked California best. California has those giant redwoods that make you dream of dinosaurs and saber-toothed tigers. I ended up in Stockton State Hospital, after I told the doctor I thought my head was made of glass. I slept on a straw mat in an eggshell room and ate bean soup morning, noon, and night. Sometimes they served cold coffee. Mother found me in California and took me back by train to Boston.

Irene's meeting me tonight to square dance in the ballroom. She promised. She has Christmas-red hair and lives in the women's wing up on the third floor. I live in the men's basement. I guess you could say I've practiced square dancing already this week. I had six partners yesterday in the Therapy Room—four held me down as my legs kicked and arms twitched. Two cradled my head. The past seems a blur but I can't forget Irene. She's my shining star. She hates it if I buck my hips when I'm holding her close. "Never do that again," she scolds, "it reminds me of my old man." I tell her I'll stop because my head could crack and my brains spill out if she shouts too loud.

CONTROLLING THE WEATHER

JEN SAYS she can control the weather. She likes making it sunny when it's supposed to be cloudy. If rain's predicted she'll pray and turn it dry as a bone. She drives weathermen crazy. Her specialty's Indian summer. Even in the dead of winter she'll summon a heat blast.

She's not sure how she received this power but thinks it's her connection to God. She's never missed Mass since First Holy Communion and tears up when talking about Jesus. If it does snow she claims she willed that too because looking out at the falling flakes makes her feel cozy inside her room at the ward.

INCARCERATION

I DRIVE BY where they hold you. Your campus resembles a business park—concrete cubes sporting thin vertical windows. Glass ink black, yet I can see my car passing through. You're tucked in the Theo Lacy wing. Grounds boast resort-green lawns, eucalyptus, roses in raised beds.

Across the street, the ash trees bend. Hydrants are milky-white. Chain-wire fences enclose a field with blue end zones. Goal posts the color of hydrants. Remember your touchdown in the big game? The cheerleaders loved you.

I hang a left and head back to the freeway. Clouds kill the sun. Shadows roll over the forgotten and tumble into the sea.

ELDER CARE

MARK STICKS his mother Mary in a kennel beside the television. It's the best solution, he thinks, easier than having her run loose around the house getting into trouble. Once he caught her painting on the wall like Rembrandt. Another time she was out back chewing a daffodil. "Bad Mummy," Mark scolded. Mary's grown accustomed to the cramped kennel quarters and spends most of her time dreaming. Sometimes Mark sees her kicking legs and flailing arms as if she's running.

Mark keeps the curtains closed. He feeds Mary macaroni & cheese out of his dead dog's bowl morning, noon, and night. A special treat is chili. Once in a blue moon Mary gets barbecue. She laps water from a teacup. He takes her for walks in the backyard using her new rhinestone collar. She lifts her leg over jasmine. "Good Mummy," says Mark, "let it all out." He opens the curtains every full moon, weeps in his boyhood room as Mary claws the kennel and howls.

BARBECUED TOAD

I'M HURLING koa chairs at Troy, my big brother. He's using the cover of the Weber Kettle like a shield and deflects the chairs, one after another.

I'm mad at him for feeding my cats barbecued toad—two are puking at the high tide line. When I run out of chairs, he tongs fresh toads on the grill and starts whistling to the tune of "Aloha 'Oe." I grab a paddle from an outrigger canoe. I'm surprised how light and good the paddle feels. I slash at the air with the blade.

"Stop!" he goes, ducking my first swing.

"Strike one," I say as I move in close to the croaking kettle.

MEAT OF MACHINES

DADIO REFUSES Gert, my mother's mother, private nurses. Next thing we know, he packs her off to the Goddard House, way over in Jamaica Plain.

It's raining when we visit. Hallways reek of chlorine. "Halp, halp!" spills down the corridor. We find Gert in bed, dipping cornbread in her chowder. A nurse charges in with pills. "Funny things go on here," June Spoon whispers. "Tough," goes Dadio, "we're broke."

"Depends catches most everythin'," Gert announces.

Very next day, Dadio loses heavy in the market. Then comes blood in the stool, transfusions, a major reconstruction. Dadio lies tubed in ICU, meat of machines, a surgeon's recreation. He sucks oxygen through a keyhole in his neck.

"Keep me alive," go his eyes, "keep me alive."

THE REST HOME

I'M AT GERT'S rest home in Jamaica Plain. June Spoon's in another state, but wants to talk to Gert. Gert sits in a wheelchair. The rest home doesn't have a phone. Knobs come out of the wall. I adjust the knobs to hear incoming calls. June Spoon's voice comes in garbled, and adjusting the knobs doesn't help. A nurse watches. Then I hear Dadio—he says wheel Gert over to the TV because Troy has a way to communicate through HBO. "Do they have HBO?" Dadio asks. The nurse nods. "Gert sucks eggs!" goes Troy through the television, even though it's not on. "Hear your brother?" Dadio asks. "Yes," I say, but then the nurse wheels Gert back to bed. "She's too tired for games," the nurse tells me.

Next thing I know, June Spoon's at the rest home. She's holding her mother, rocking her back and forth in bed. "Mumsy," June Spoon coos, "Mumsy Wumsy." Gert's face has been made up—Oil of Olay, lipstick, rouge. She looks as if she's in her 50s, not her 90s. "What a terrific job," June Spoon says. Then Gert stands up on the bed and starts bouncing. The feathers in the pillows come out. Feathers stick to her oily skin, hair, and black leotard. Soon she looks as if she's wearing a bird costume. Gert jumps off the bed and chases me. "Mumsy!" June Spoon belts. I run the corridor and am amazed how

45

fast Gert is. I hop onto an escalator. I'm in a shopping mall and Gert watches me rise from the floor of Macy's. The escalator lifts me up, up into the clouds.

EATING GLASS

I'M EATING GLASS in my dream. I enjoy blue glass best, especially indigo. I buy chunks at Home Depot, not panes or sheets or anything, just bite-sized pieces. Cubed beads are delicious. So are pink crystal dolphins and green sharks. I get excited sucking on tiny glass planes, cars and boats. I love running my tongue over the forms of creatures and things before chomping down. My dream girlfriend says eating glass will kill me. Still, my stomach feels fine. I carry lunch in a brown paper bag down to the boardwalk after the surfers leave. I pull a glass turtle out of the bag, hold it up to the sun. Dadio glares in the violet shell.

THE RETURN OF WIGTON

MRS. WIGTON STARTS talking to herself the day her husband dies. Her conversations include how to poison weeds, the meaning of dials on her Buick's dash, and what to have for dinner.

On the first anniversary of his death, Wigton walks through the front door in his suit. He sits down at the dinner table, where his wife is drinking merlot. Wigton's slightly grayer and a bit leaner but nonetheless in fine spirits.

"Where have you been?" Mrs. Wigton demands.

"To see God," Wigton answers.

Mrs. Wigton blesses the bread and passes it. "How is He?" she whispers.

"Shorter than you think." Wigton rips the loaf, studies the halves, then stuffs the big one deep in his mouth.

GHOSTS

FLAGS FLY half-mast. Down on the shore, a priest shovels sand while the wind kicks up. Umbrellas lose their moorings, float overturned on the sea. Snack on green mangoes and dream of trees covered in crows. The crows will soon land on your roof. Be patient—fruit blooms after midnight. A rat scales the jacaranda, performs a balancing act on the feeder. He's after black seeds. Your parents? They'll disappear the way their parents did. This avenue is a circus of shadows—the street cleaner can't scrub them away. "Three Blind Mice" plays as the ice cream truck circles the block. A pink balloon, turned ashen, drifts for the sun.

FEEDING THE BIRDS

I'M STANDING at the screen door of my parent's old bedroom: June Spoon's out back with the birds. There's the usual riot of chirps. "Plenty for all," she promises, under-handing like a softball pitcher. June Spoon looks silly tossing in a pink muumuu and heels. She throws pieces of stale hotdog buns, scattering widely over the lawn. Even doves have a chance. "You've had enough," she tells an aggressive myna. The doves are her favorites. Once she got a crush on a mallard and bought him his own bag of birdseed. She believes a crimson cardinal with a bum leg is the second coming of Popsy. "Here's some for you," she beckons a skinny sparrow.

A plastic litter box filled with water is perched on a stone. When the cat died the birds got a birdbath. Toads love it. The birds won't bathe or even drink if the toads are swimming. "You get out," June Spoon scolds.

"Did you see you-know-who?" I ask when she comes inside.

"No," she answers, lowering her eyes. Her hair is as white as an egret.

"Maybe he's on vacation."

She nods and offers a smile. "Popsy sure liked to travel."

I see hopping outside—a black toad bounces over the grass like a crazed shadow. I think he's heading for the ferns. A family of apricot finches takes flight.

OCEAN VIEW

A PRIEST on the beach digs with a chrome shovel. Blue water shivers behind him. Anne, my sister, drowned when she was three. Whenever I float on my back I hear Anne calling my name. "Hoy," she goes, "Hoy Hoy!" She calls from a castle made of pearls under the sea. See that? The birthmark on my calf is expanding. A ladybug buzzes the window like a fly. Do I keep her in or release the luck? I slide the glass open. The blade of the shovel sticks in the sand. Better to have a beach full of luck than hog it for myself. Trouble—my glass mermaid arrives cracked in the mail. I am human, somewhere beyond repair.

UNDERGROUND PARKING

IT'S PALM SUNDAY. I accompany June Spoon underground, into the bowels of a parking structure. She admits it's her fantasy to be kidnapped by a celebrity on a Sunday before Mass. "Why on a Sunday?" I ask. "That will be the best excuse to miss Mass," she replies. "Why don't you just stay home?" "And have God send me straight to Hell?" she goes. "No, thank-you." We reach her Mercedes classic with paint as blue as a robin's egg. June Spoon wants to be buried in this car, instead of a coffin. She says ending up in something familiar will be good for her soul. She flops down in the suicide seat. "Luck Be a Lady" plays on the radio. "Get in back," June Spoon instructs. I swing open the back door and climb in. Frank Sinatra sits behind the wheel. He fires up the Mercedes, reverses. "We going to Mass?" I ask. "No," June Spoon answers, "I'm busy getting kidnapped." Frank kisses her hard on the lips and floors it.

BONES

MOST WOMEN HATE bones. They recoil biting fragments stuck in meat. "You're carving all wrong," my wife scolds. For women, bones flash the chain of life: birthing in fields; sucking on teats; playing till the sun sets; getting trucked to the slaughterhouse at the edge of town.

Men don't mind bones. Whenever I hit a frag, I spit it out like a bullet. Perhaps bones link us to our primal pasts, such as hunting mammoths with spears on icy plains. The women imagine death back at the cave, learn how to whisper. A girl drags a charred bone over the wall.

BOOK 4

CREATURE COMFORTS

URGES

MY THREE-YEAR-OLD'S been neutered but he still has urges. He gets on top of my plush bear, sinks canines into the soft head, and drags the bear over the mattress bucking his hips. It's somewhat lewd. It's been happening daily and I pray he doesn't do this in front of my girlfriend or parents. Still, I feel bad for him.

I call his lover Honey Bear. She looks like she's been around the block. Sometimes I watch him dream—eyelids fluttering, whiskers quivering—and imagine he's playing with five plush children.

SPINNING AT THE ASYLUM

TODAY IS Irene's third operation. "This time women's troubles," Nurse Croner whispers. I pick Irene a bouquet of pink and yellow roses from the bushes outside Hooper Hall. Thorns cut my fingers. Ernie the Attendant scolds me for stealing, says next time he'll drown me in Bladder Pond. I'm not allowed to visit Irene so the bouquet winds up in the Day Room for everyone to enjoy.

Doc decides I need more blood to the brain. I tell him it's not good to move blood around and that too much blood could crack my glass head. "Nonsense," he says. I enter the Therapy Room. Ernie lifts me into a chair hanging from the ceiling and straps me in. Doc pulls on a blindfold—soft cotton feels good over my eyes. Ernie sneezes. The chair starts to turn so I grab the steel posts rising out of the armrests. Soon I'm spinning like a top. Why, it feels just like I'm back at the Boston Fair riding the Moonrocket with Dads. "Hang on tight, son," Dads warns, "hang on for your life!"

HAZEL

SHE SPOTS HIM beside the acacia in employee parking. He reminds her of Hazel in *Watership Down*. He looks skinny. An urge to leave food hits but she realizes he'll grow dependent and, if she ever moved on, he'd die of starvation. But she figures a few organic veggies wouldn't hurt. After work on Friday, she places her offering on the grass beside the bush. "Hazel," she calls, "sweet little Hazel." She returns to her car and scouts: a nose and twitching ears poke out of the acacia. He darts, grabs a julienned carrot, and disappears into his sanctuary. Several minutes pass and Hazel returns for a second. She starts her car and heads for the freeway.

It becomes customary for her to leave carrots every day after work, and routine for her to watch. One afternoon he doesn't show. "Oh, Hazel," she coos from the driver's seat, "where's my sweet little Hazel?" She waits until the lot empties. Still no Hazel. A crow lands near the carrots—she scares it off by opening and slamming the door. An hour passes and the carrots still haven't been touched. She remembers all the cats and dogs she's adopted over the years: most were strays or humane society lifers. She takes the long way home over the bridge, turning left on the county road. She powers her windows down. The road skirts an avocado grove and she slows for a stand. A family mills around the bins and crates. A boy hugs his mother. She speeds up, crying as wind whips through her windows.

SAFE AND PERFECTLY NORMAL

BURT'S OUTBOUND 727 popped through the marine layer like a Champagne cork—an inbound Cessna nearly clipped the jet's roof. "Jesus!" Burt squealed. The seat next to him was empty. The woman across the aisle had on a headset. The pilot issued no just-missed-killing-you apology and not a single passenger registered a reaction. "Blind as bats," Burt mumbled in his window seat. Sometimes, when he was this high up, he thought about the afterlife. He pictured living on a cloud with his dead parents and with all the pets he'd buried or cremated over the years. There'd been a golden he liked better than his old man, a pup he saved after it got caught in a rip at Maverick's. He rustled the *Wall Street Journal*—gold was up but Microsoft was taking a dump. He made a mental note to max out his Roth IRA. He turned his attention to the overhead screen—a rerun of *30 Rock* played. Alec Baldwin looked fat. Fat and old. He was certain Alec dyed his hair. At times he felt he could pass for one of the Baldwin brothers and vowed to hit the gym hard after his 49th birthday. The captain came on and said they'd touch down in half-an-hour. He stared out the window at the 101. The freeway was a conveyor belt of shiny cars and trucks. They reminded him of M&M's. Becky was one of those M&M's and she'd be waiting in baggage claim. He guzzled coffee. He promised himself not to mention the near miss. It would only upset Becky. An upset Becky wouldn't want sex. He imagined plucking his bag off the carousel, draping an arm over his wife's shoulder, and heading north on the 101. Traffic would be light and he'd surprise her by stopping at Il Fornaio for lunch. They'd sip pinot noir and order the seafood fettuccini. The wheels hit. The jet glided across the tarmac and the captain warned everyone to keep seat belts secure. "Sheeple," Burt muttered, unfastening. He felt good back home in San Francisco. It would be great seeing Becky. He was fairly certain it would be another safe and perfectly normal day.

THE MOVIES

IT'S ALL been planned: the man you identify with is the underdog. You don't envy his life but you root for him anyway because you've been squashed in similar ways, although less exaggerated. Millions of men watch this movie and most will identify too, especially when the violins and cellos play after he lands that special woman. You're lucky. You've absorbed a man's challenge and sexual triumph in about two hours. You feel good strolling the lobby past arcade boys sweating joysticks as men move silently through the turnstiles.

TO A FRIEND AT THE BEN HUR APARTMENTS

A CATARACT SKY on Hyde. Something flies by—an albatross or a plane. You're up on the 6th floor where the bed bugs live. I like Ben Hur's cobalt canopy. A boy in jeans enters the shade, searches the list of dwellers. Salt greens your buzzer. Don't miss his shy ring boiling water for Earl Grey.

I have seen your BVDs tumble dry at Dair's Speedy Wash. You buy cognac at Serve Well Market. Cigars at Mini Smoke Shoppe. Your voice drags Sunday mornings, when we sip espresso at breeze window watching our city shrink to a village. Smell ocean? Below us, the escape ladder slants 60 degrees. Traffic's one way. A loose dog pisses a hydrant.

WETLANDS

MEN LIVING in the Palo Alto wetlands use disposable diapers to keep themselves warm. Their campfire rages across the street from the city dump. There's that vinegar smell of newborns. Winter threatens from the south. A moonless night discourages clouds. The top half of the world has blown off, letting in the stars. Men wrap diapers around their shoulders, like grandmothers with knitted shawls.

MORNING FLIGHT TO CHICAGO

CLOUDS? Nonexistent. How does that yellow tape stay stuck to the wing? The sky is empty, except for this plane. The ground is empty too—no homes, no freeways, no malls. I see no rivers or lakes. Craters merge with rusty scars and dirt roads resembling veins. "Death croissant?" the blonde stewardess asks. I nod and she hands me a bag. The woman beside me smells of vinegar. I imagine diapers. A man unleashes his machine gun laugh at the overhead screen. The stewardess grunts wheeling her cart east. We roll on into the sun.

ON THE GROUNDS OF THE ASYLUM

THE FOUR-STORY ASYLUM blooms out of your shoulders. You carry the flagstone and brick weight well. Yes, I see your window in the basement, just below your left hand. How convenient that the Therapy Room's only a few doors down. You lean into the slope for balance, smelling of bleach. Are you wearing shades? No. Those are your deep-set eyes living in shadow. You look good in your white short-sleeve, paisley tie, white pants and shoes. The breeze curls your tie like bacon. You could pass for a doctor or, at the very least, a well-groomed attendant. That's great about square dancing Saturday night in the ballroom. I agree, you're a lady's man.

Your sisters are visiting. They sit on the lawn, cheeks fatigued from smiling without showing teeth. Gert's got on a Church hat. Virginia clutches her purse. Their lips are parched from chitchatting about Mother and Dads, even after glasses of asylum lemonade. Playing pretend is hard. "You're no son of mine," Dads had said, after catching your hand in the Nolan's Restaurant register and then under Virginia's lacy skirt.

I imagine a younger you riding the rails west, watching cities, farms, and buffalo land whiz by. You dined on pork and beans. A hobo sharing your spoon passed a corncob pipe. You reached the Pacific, ran for the blue, floated belly up fully clothed. "I'm sorry, Dads," you whispered as the tide carried you out, "I'm so so sorry."

HURRICANE IRENE

"GOODNIGHT, IRENE," he says, watching waves slam into the teeth of the pier at Myrtle Beach. Dogs jog the shore. A couple walks the sand hand-in-hand. Gulls spiral the sky. The beachfront windows of the Bar Harbor Hotel arch like tombstones. The dark horizon makes him think of Revelation and angels spilling bowls. He isn't anywhere near the hurricane, or even North Carolina for that matter. He's watching 2,200 miles away in San Diego, on an Internet cam feed he clicks to wide screen. He raises decibels to experience the full impact of the storm: he enjoys the moaning wind and the metallic clink the rain makes pelting the cam. He imagines the view from a room at the Bar Harbor. It's like a football game, pitting hurricane against pier. Nature vs. man. An unstoppable force meeting an immovable object. He turns a fan on high and pretends the room's window is open. The breeze makes him feel he as though he's really there. He sees a woman standing at the water's edge, searching for something in the waves.

DODO THE CAT

EVERYONE HAS a book out these days, including my cat Dodo. She writes couplets about being mistreated, not getting three squares, and being on a diet. Another big gripe is getting cooped up all day in the apartment while I'm at work. What can I do? Dodo should realize someone needs to bring home the bacon on wet days when the world is mute and the only sounds are birds at the feeder and rain on the roof.

DANNY BOY

THE MAN ABOVE ME calls for his dog. His dachshund has slipped through the black bars of the wrought-iron fence separating our properties. "Daniel," he goes, "oh, Danny Boy."

I don't mind people giving their dogs human names. It's kind of cute actually. But what's not cute is how Daniel, or Danny Boy, is digging through my meadow of poppies and Indian paintbrush from Crater Lake. Jesus, that damn Danny's sending up a cascade of petals and roots as he rips through my beauties.

"Daniel," the man continues, "come here now!" A woman joins him at the fence. They peer into my property looking for their little bastard. Hawks circle. Daniel quits digging, runs back to the fence, and squeezes through the bars. The woman picks him up and rocks him like a baby. "Bad dog," she scolds. They return to their house, with her still cradling the dachshund and the man hovering close.

Tomorrow, I'll hike up my hill to survey the damage. Perhaps I can make a poppy-paintbrush bouquet and ring their doorbell. Funny, I don't even know their names. But I do know Daniel, or Danny Boy, and already miss his visit.

SUNRISE AT CRATER LAKE, OREGON

GHOST CLOUDS hug Danger Bay. The retired carry drip coffee in cups, claim a row of pine rockers overlooking the crater. Hickory creaks like bones. Snow geese glide the spruce as Watchman Peak ignites. "Here we go," says safari-hatted man. Llao's Fingers reach for the Phantom Ship shadows. The rim drops its reverse image into the water—upside down ponderosas appear in the lake. A Bostonian texts her grandson while the sun greens the hemlocks on Wizard Island. "Incoming," calls safari-hatted man. A platoon of yellow warblers lands on the lodge's façade, pecks salt off the lava. There's the wild smell of feathers. An eagle circles the riot of beaks.

notes:

Llao's Fingers: fingerlike patterns on the lake's surface made by the spirit of the slain god of the lake

Phantom Ship: tiny island resembling a pirate ship 2 miles northeast of Wizard Island

BOOK 5

SLAUGHTERHOUSE FLIES

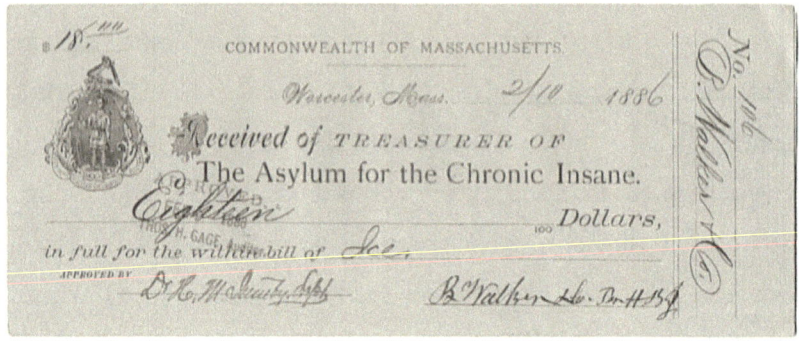

MESSAGES FROM THE WEST

THIS NEW BABY card says on the back it's printed on recycled paper. If I hold it up to the light just right I can make out the Obits from the *L.A. Times*, January something, 1969.

A black-and-white cat waits for a white man to stop at a Portland intersection before crossing in front of his Volvo. A black woman coming from the opposite direction on a 10-speed slows down to admire the crossing cat. Man and woman exchange glances. So, the three finally reunite at this intersection in Oregon—a white man in a car, a black woman on a bike, and a black-and-white cat on foot. The cat is actually the man's child he had with the woman years ago, a baby they agreed to give up for adoption because she was much too young and he, the driver, refused to marry her because he already had a wife and kittens in another state.

A doe lies on the shoulder of Freeway 280, just south of Burlingame. She wails beneath the diamond sign with a buck silhouette that says, WATCH FOR DEER NEXT 13 MILES.

A San Francisco man decides to retire from his job as a down-and-out fixture in the park across the street from City Hall. He rolls all the shopping carts he has collected over the years to Gert's Grocery and gets on average 25-bucks-a-cart, depending of course on degree of rust. He uses the money to buy an Olds convertible he found the day before at Omar's Used Chariots. It's the same car his father drove in East Lansing, exactly thirty years ago. After crossing the Golden Gate Bridge, the man adjusts his rearview mirror while speeding home to Michigan, his convertible top down.

A newcomer to the island of Moloka'i builds with doors facing east and west instead of the customary north and south. Locals worry about her safety. They warn the woman that on full moons the Night Marchers, ghosts from Old Hawaii, come down from the mountains to go fishing. These ghosts follow traditional north-south paths. If the doors are not consistent with these paths her house will be a box with no way out. The woman laughs. She tells the locals they're overly superstitious. The first night in her new home, the moon is full. Dogs don't bark. Instead, they howl. A lavender ring surrounds the moon. The woman has a pleasant sleep. She dreams she's at a great feast on the beach, like a clambake back in Boston. A man comes out of the sea and approaches her. She's intrigued. He's holding something red. When she wakes, an `äweoweo rests on her pillow—its giant eye staring up.

note:

`äweoweo: also known as the Hawaiian Bigeye, this red nocturnal fish with huge eyes hides out in caves and under reef ledges during the day

EYE DOC

I LIMP SHORT, ghost calves straining. Cane propels through electric doors. Glass and rubber seal me inside. Smells of salt, baking plastic.

Patients numb as goldfish. Summer leaks through skylights. Where the hell is Suite D?

I wait behind cataract grandma. Drug salesmen gossip like Mormons. Plaque says *Dr. Robert P. Mudd*. Paintings of villas with cows and vineyards.

Grapes ripe, staring like eyes.

THE DISEASE

IT FORCED YOU up in the dark morning. It made you take a hard look at your life. It was awful. It was how a lawyer reviews a case and decides the case is lost. It was a plague. People from Boston to Beijing, Honolulu to Helsinki, North Pole to South, suffered. Depression tormented every neighborhood of every city of every continent. The world deteriorated. Dolphins washed up on beaches. Dumps stretched fists of garbage into the clouds. An evil halo circled Earth.

A company invented Kicki, a pill you popped before sleep. It kept all the bad feelings jailed in dreams. The governments approved the drug with no red tape. Citizens took Kicki and woke refreshed. Some were so happy they gave up coffee and cocaine. The evil halo turned invisible. New Yorkers designed a giant balloon in the drug's likeness and floated it down Fifth Avenue on Thanksgiving Day.

The world was not such a bad place, as long as you took Kicky. Soon almost everyone had the disease. Kicki parties became the rage. The governments relaxed guidelines so you could get it over-the-counter and from vending machines.

Rebels wanted to experience the disease. They asked questions like "What *is* the purpose of life?" The media stopped the interviews. The governments called them "nihilists." The rebels were rounded up by the police and force-fed Kicki. The ones who hid the drug under their tongues had their tongues removed.

And the Earth was a better place—diseased, yes—but a planet full of hopeful, industrious people.

KIRBY WRIGHT

CRAB NEWBURG

I MAKE CRAB Newburg and serve it on a picnic table in the backyard. The Newburg is canary yellow. Guess I overdid it on the eggs. Dadio leaves the table. I ladle the Newburg out, serving it in clear glass bowls. First I serve June Spoon, then her friend Eleanor. Eleanor died last March. "Do they have restaurants in Heaven?" June Spoon asks. I'm embarrassed when my mother talks with yellow on her tongue. Eleanor makes fists, pounds them on the table. "Bring out the shells," she says.

I return to the kitchen, where flies orbit the crab stink counter. I begin stacking the shells. Dadio stirs his martini with a middle finger while thrusting his pelvis back and forth. He's suddenly 30 years younger. "Son," he goes, "in the old days, I used to screw Eleanor." "Would you do her now?" I ask. He stares out the window. "Not when she's a zombie," he mumbles. Dadio ages 30 years the second he steps out of the kitchen. "Where are those shells?" Eleanor calls from the backyard.

THE QUEEN OF ABOVE AVERAGE POETRY

YOU'VE READ HER. She's everywhere: journals, anthologies, collections, online, offline, the walls of public restrooms. Omnipresent as god. Her lines are somewhere between fake deep and brilliant. Sometimes her endings stun me. Sometimes they don't. I picture her scribbling furiously on a big wide bed, the bridge of owl-eye glasses hugging her nose. "Where is my tea?" she calls out. An assistant downstairs busies herself making Earl Grey and cataloguing contributor copies that have arrived by post. The assistant notices something crawling the carpet, a spider, a daddy longlegs she's certain the Queen of Above Average Poetry will never see.

IT MAKES YOUR EARS RING

MINUTES BEFORE you die, you'll hear what sounds like a car alarm blocks away. Next comes the sound of a trumpet, closer. "The boy playing next door," you smile. Then comes the sound of rain on the roof. But it's not raining. The aroma of bacon drifts in through the screen. Cats and dogs ignore you.

Flash to a service with sad, impatient faces. The trumpet taps. "Fast how it goes," you whisper. Watch them file out after small talk and prayers. Attend a reception at the old home, where your family serves eggplant, cubed cheeses, chocolate chip cookies. The trumpet now sounds like a siren—it makes your ears ring as you skim an indigo sky into the sun.

ONWARD TO CASTLE LAKE

I STROLL infinity road through oak, tripping over a drainage ditch made of wood. Thrushes scurry through the forest. A caretaker passes cradling a pitchfork. I reach a gazebo with support posts disguised as scrolls and a ceiling frescoed with newborns. Babies with the faces of old men. One squeezes a bug-eyed carp. Rococo clamshells and grape leaf garlands. Onward. The oaks become giants, mist swirling trunks the size of redwoods. Limbs arch the road, creating a tunnel.

I reach a tiny dock. The lake is before me—a jade square with lily pads riding its surface. There's an island of birch. A rowboat, tethered by frayed rope to the dock, lies frozen in water. The boat's floor glitters korunas. Footsteps. Are those feet? No, just oaks on the road dropping acorns. The boat rocks. The White Lady stands on a lily pad. She's wearing a bone-white dress with gold fringe. The sash around her waist is strung with keys. "Hey, babe," I greet. She pulls on a pair of black gloves. "Babe?" I go. A breeze kicks up—the lake shivers. I smell fireplaces, the stench of dungeons, stale mead.

ARTHRITIS

BURT HATED being in bed like this, crippled by arthritis. It had invaded both feet and the pills weren't helping. He'd overdone it again on the running. Nobody in his family had arthritis and he wondered why god had cursed him with it. "Sonuvabitch," he mumbled. He was so frustrated he wanted to cut his feet off. He imagined fusing steel wheels to bone and racing in 5 and 10Ks, even half-marathons. "Fast as lightning," he smiled, seeing himself in an expansive trophy room with a girl in shorts at his side. Why, he might even have a shot at the Olympics.

He heard his wife Becky downstairs. She was preparing dinner. The fridge made a sucking noise, followed by the utensil drawer clanging open. Becky was making soup and sandwiches. She hated to cook. He knew she hated waiting on him, going up the stairs with food and down with empty bowls and plates.

"Honey," Burt called.

There was a metallic clink, one that sounded like a spoon striking tile. "What?" Becky finally answered.

"Bring me the hacksaw."

LAMB

THIS LAMB has an old taste, not rotten or anything, just beyond gamey. It's a putrid flavor, something garlic and oregano can't disguise. Maybe I should have baked it longer.

Vonnegut told me the creative brain's baked by 55. That's the right side I guess. That means my mind's already half-dead and years past gamey.

I apply mint jelly—that gives the lamb a snap of freshness. I think of a playful creature as I chew, one springing up a bright green hill to greet its mother.

LAST RITES

I WONDER what time of the day or night I'll die. I'm a late sleeper so I don't want to go too early. After my afternoon Reuben might be best, say an hour before the local news. But it could be morning, when a rooster crows as a jet's shadow drowns the house. I imagine Last Rites while I sit on the throne. Father Keelan's out there right now, sliding prayers under the door.

SLAUGHTERHOUSE FLIES

MY BODY'S in that big steel cabinet, in the drawer tagged with my name second from the bottom. Yes, slide it open. Voilà my shaved and deodorized carcass, the remnants of our loveless marriage. I look alive, don't I? I'm a miracle of hospital refrigeration. I still need nose hairs clipped and glossed lips so I look good at the service. No, don't tip the morgue boy. And don't bring your new man to Church. We don't want people talking, gossip thick as slaughterhouse flies.

THE GREAT OAK

IT WAS A SCORCHING summer and the great oak was dying. Ferns drowned in a cascade of leaves. Frogs fled. Birds didn't land on bare branches. A boy tied a leaf to a pole and held it up to shade a bough. 'It's the least I can do," he thought. The boy knew the great oak had provided shade for years, maybe even centuries, and it was time to give back. Children playing in the forest saw the boy and spread the word: all the boys and girls in the village started searching for poles. When the poles ran out they searched for sticks. Soon the tree was sheltered from the sun. A girl raised her voice in song and the children joined in. Leaves quit falling as the great oak listened.

LEG OF JEN

MY PARENTS are having my sister's leg for dinner. June Spoon asks if I'm hungry and I tell her no, that I just pigged out at McDonald's. Dadio scolds me for filling up on junk food. "No room in the inn?" June Spoon jokes. Dadio lips smack a hunk of hindquarter. "Succulent," he hums, "you don't know what you're missing." Funny, he never said that when my calf was the main course for Easter. I think it was too tough to chew. The thing that bugs Dadio is sitting down to eat yourself—it's as if he thinks you've turned lazy and should be busy making new parts.

I hobble up the hall. I find my kid sister in her room, in bed under the sheets. It smells of piss and blood. The tiles are covered with sequins that will become scales for a Halloween costume. "No din din?" I ask. Jen tells me she's lost her appetite and wouldn't eat herself anyway, even if it does annoy Dadio. She says he took both legs, that her left's in the freezer. I check out Bob, her four-foot boa, which she keeps in a glass terrarium propped on a chest of drawers. Bob looks much smaller coiled on river stones.

"How will you get around, Jen?" I ask. "I'll manage," she answers, "don't you?" I tell her yes. Then I realize she's hiding her body. I'd forgotten Dadio took an arm on Independence Day. She adapted like a champ to an artificial one with robotic features clad in fleshy silicone. Still, it's a pity she has only one limb. "Never let them get the other arm," I caution. "Oh, no," she goes, "they're saving that for Christmas." Jen gazes at the terrarium. She asks me what's on the menu tomorrow and sighs in relief when I answer "chops." Dadio prefers lamb when he's not gnawing on us. My sis tells me she'll learn how to slither by studying Bob, when he hunts mice in his glass cage. She promises to be as mobile as Bob, maybe even better, and might slither down the hall toward chops.

BOOK 6

NOTES FROM THE FRONT LINE

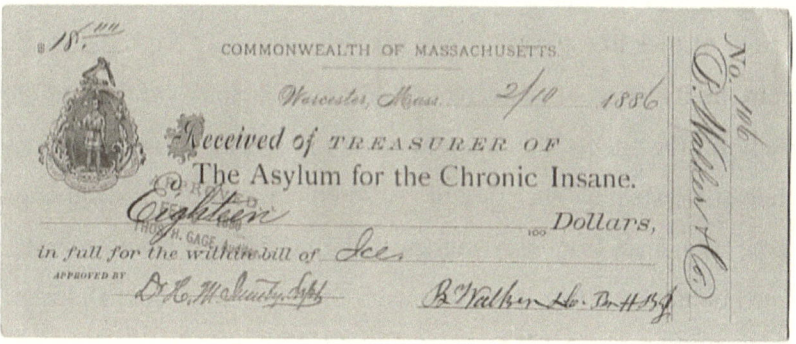

TOY SOLDIERS

HERE ARE THE ENEMY lines, bristling with killers armed with guns, swords, and spears. Neat rows stretch from the doorway across a field of tiles to the edge of the rug. It's an assault from the south, from the direction of the parents' bedroom. The boy's tin troops are ready for the enemy's charge, their rows facing the door. Both sides are battle-tested. Neither side has suffered major casualties, although some bear scars from slashing and stabbing. Several have lost eyes. One hobbles on a peg leg fashioned from a Popsicle stick. But most remain whole. The boy plans on stretching his second line and wrapping them around so, after the first assault, he can swing men around the edges and attack from the rear. "Trapped," he smiles.

He speaks as Captain Bricker, his side's leader. He picks up his favorite soldier, a man whose nose was cleaved only last week. "Ready on the front line, Lieutenant Trax?" he asks. "Ready," Trax replies. "Hold your ground till my signal." Trax salutes. "Will do, Captain." He sticks Trax back in front. He knows his lieutenant's vulnerable but he's willing to risk his safety for the good of the army.

The boy needs to win. He's already lost too many fights. He can't control the skirmishes beyond the doorway, struggles lost when the belt plays taps on his backside and cries for mercy echo off the redwood walls. Saturdays scare him most, when the sun is hot and bottles gather on the table outside. He hates the patio. That's Dadio's place, one that smells of cut grass, burnt oil, and beer. The boy wishes for Sunday. He wants a fat newspaper delivered, funnies to share, a chance to make Dadio smile.

THE GIRL

THE GIRL FEARS death. It is something she doesn't understand, the thing reported nightly in the living room—Americans stuffed in body bags and Vietnamese stacked like cords of wood along the muddy roads. When the girl asks, her father tells her there is no God. He wants to kill the innocence in her, to make her grow up. He puts down *Scientific American* and turns off the light. He leaves the room. The girl cries in the dark, her tears hitting the love seat. She feels distance, as if watching herself through a telescope.

The father knows she is crying. It is for the best, he thinks, climbing the stairs to bed. He doesn't look back. It is a gentle killing, humane, one that fits the conscience of a man who experiments on mice. He is skilled at murdering the mice sweetly, a little at a time, in the glass cage back at the lab.

The girl will grow in the darkness the father has built.

HAPPY 50TH

YOU INSIST it's an exercise in forgiveness. Still, you don't pick up the phone to wish step mom happy birthday. Maybe it has something to do with your father, the way he uses her to shield himself from you. Or is it the promise she broke about paying for college? It's obvious your voices will never touch as step mom tears in smoke rolling over 50 candles.

THE BRACELET

DADIO STROLLS Fort Street Mall in downtown Honolulu. He stops to admire a silver bracelet in the window at Sasaki Jewelers. It features after-the-harvest scenes with a couple dancing while farmers play flutes and fiddles. A wolfish dog howls at the moon. He goes in. "Da kine 925 pure," says Mr. Sasaki, handing it over. It's heavier than he expected. And wider. It reminds him of a shackle with its U-shaped design and interlocking clasp. He likes the clinking sound it makes opening and closing. He tries slipping it over his wrist but it won't fit. "Fo' *haole* girl," advises Mr. Sasaki. Dadio thinks this is the perfect gift to show June his affection, something not as serious as an engagement ring yet substantial enough to demonstrate his powerful love. He imagines her opening his package in her hometown of Boston. He sniffs the bracelet—it smells like blood. "She love you long time," promises the jeweler. Dadio reaches for his wallet, smiling.

note:

haole: white

FIRST CRUSH

THE BOY LOVED Barbies. His sister's collection included Sparkle Beach Barbie, French Maid Barbie, Red Moon Barbie, Dallas Cheerleaders Barbie, and Supergirl Barbie. He liked Sparkle Beach Barbie best, mostly because she was tan and looked hot in her gold lamé bikini. She made him think of shorelines and coconuts. One day, when his sister was at Chuck E. Cheese's, he whisked Sparkle Beach Barbie off to his bedroom. He locked the door, flopped on the bed, and kissed her. Then he buried his nose in her vanilla hair. She smelled good. She smelled as good as the insides of his mother's new Buick. He slipped off her gold bottoms and tongued her. "Yum," he said. He imagined her moaning. He slicked her long legs wet with his tongue. He heard the Buick pull up and buried her under the covers. That night he dreamt he was a man doll driving through a toy town with Sparkle Beach Barbie at his side. They stopped for chocolate cake pulled warm out of an Easy-Bake Oven.

The next morning, his father found Sparkle Beach Barbie on the boy's floor with her legs spread. "Playing with dolls now?" he asked. "No," the boy answered. "I've got my eye on you," his father warned.

The boy's sister found out. She called him a kidnaper. She started keeping her Barbies under lock and key in a cedar chest. "He's just going through a phase," he heard his mother say over the phone. The boy bought his own Sparkle Beach Barbie at Toys "R" Us, after telling the pimply-faced clerk the doll was a gift for his kid sister. He hid Barbie under the mattress and pulled her out when everyone went to sleep. He kissed her all over and prayed that, one day, he would find a real live girl just like her to marry. His johnson throbbed. Then something strange happened—the boy realized Sparkle Beach Barbie was a dead ringer for his mother. Younger, yes, but cut from the same cloth. Same hair color. Same pert breasts. He remembered his mother lying out in her gold bikini down by the shore rubbing lotion on her long legs. It had smelled like coconuts. She'd passed him the tube and he squirted creamy goo over her back and shoulders. "Sick!" the boy said, leaping out of bed. Barbie went flying. His underpants were wet, sticky. His feet felt welded to the cold tile.

THE VOICES OF ANGELS

JUNE SPOON WALTZES into the kitchen while her boys are disciplined in their rooms. She opens the fridge to see if she needs milk. She tries figuring out which son's getting it by the pitch of the scream. "I'm sorry, Dadio," she hears as leather smacks flesh with heartbeat rhythm, "I'm so so sorry!" That's the older, June Spoon thinks. Dramatic contralto. The younger? Pure mezzo-soprano. Voices break through redwood to echo down the narrow hall. They remind her of choirboys singing at gothic cathedrals in London and Rome. "The voices of angels," June Spoon whispers, shaking the milk carton.

FLASHLIGHTING THE CREATORS

I SHINE my flashlight at their bedroom knob. Troy sticks the tip of a steak knife into the lock and turns. The lock pops. He opens and I take aim. "Cheesus," comes Dadio's voice. I ignite him as he hustles around the bed, a towel draping his waist. "Get the hell out!" he says with his *ule* bulging the terrycloth. Troy slinks off. I light up the bed—June Spoon's in the middle, pillows under her *okole* and legs spread. She's watching shadows peel the ceiling. In the background, salmon curtains smother the glass. It smells like *kumu*. "You'll get yours," Dadio promises, slamming. I use the flashlight to find my room. I keep the door open. For some reason their curtains remind me of the ones at Kaimuki Theater. I wonder how many more minutes will pass before June Spoon escapes, tiptoeing past wedding pictures down the narrow hall.

notes:

kumu: goatfish

okole: butt

ule: penis

THE LAND WITHOUT PARENTS

DADIO'S NERVOUS watching TV. He keeps crossing and uncrossing his legs on the couch. He's a lawyer, so I know he carries a boatload of stress. He starts rubbing his nuts through his shorts. It's always a low rub, one that doesn't involve the penis. I'm not sure why he's so nervous on Sunday, especially since the sports guy's doing the scores from games already played. It's as if Dadio's nuts are his magic lantern and he's trying to summon the genie to change the scores. Boy, can he rub.

"Itchy nuts?" I ask.

"Wot?" Dadio replies, sniffing his fingers.

"Nothing."

"You lil' sonuvabitch."

Strange how June Spoon never scolds Dadio. "Disgusting," she whispers in private. If it's a furious rub, she beats it and heads for the mall. Maybe June Spoon thinks men do these things to relieve tension, the way women go shopping to ease fears about losing their sex appeal.

"Goddamn 49ers," Dadio says from the couch. Now he's mixing rubs with tickles. After sniffing, he itches his nose. It's quite a production.

I wonder what effect all this has on Jen. I know she's seen him. She sees everything. Maybe it's good training for married life. She'll probably forgive her hubby for his nervous habits, even if his nuts are involved. Still, whenever Jen's near him and he starts in, I take her out to the garden. We dig for treasure in the orchid grotto. Somewhere there's a mayo bottle stuffed with monster cards, strings of plastic pearls, rhinestones, and a map to the Land Without Parents.

KID SISTER

JEN TURNS 49 tomorrow. She still lives with June Spoon at home. She frosts dark hair blonde, ignores untreated strands of silver. Cheeks? Caked foundation splashed with rouge. Red lipstick and black fingernail polish. Dragon on her left calf. She still wants to be a rock star.

Jen sleeps on a bare mattress. Pillows have no cases. Bedroom walls are the same pink I painted a half-century ago. Trolls with hair like cotton candy squat on a shelf above the dresser. She shows me an autographed glossy of Michael Jackson.

June Spoon doles out $1000/month to pay "expenses."

Romance? Jen waits for her next postcard from a grandfather married in Munich. She receives, on average, one-card-per-month. He never phones. Jen is convinced of his passion because he ends every card LOVE. She says she will marry, move to Munich, and become a celebrity on German TV.

"When's the wedding?" I ask.

"Soon," she replies.

"How soon is soon?"

She rolls her eyes. "The Year of the Pig."

I take Jen to the Punahou Carnival. She refuses to ride the Ferris Wheel. She won't play games. She spends her time searching for black dresses in white elephant and waiting in line for *malasadas*. She eats donuts with her mouth open, red lips smacking like an old woman's.

note:

malasada: Portuguese donut

STEALING THUNDER

I'M STRANGLING June Spoon in the dining room. I like the way her cheeks flush and eyes bug out. She wants to speak but can't. This must have something to do with her standing on the sidelines for years watching Dadio sing his belt on my backside. June Spoon's gurgling. I can regulate her pitch by the degree of my squeeze. A hard one brings tenor. A softie summons mezzo-soprano. I've never played a musical instrument but now I know how creating those first notes would jazz a wannabe musician. Bet I'd be a natural on the bagpipes.

I let June Spoon go. She gasps, clutching the plaster statue of Madonna with Child on the hutch. Jen appears—she's got a butter knife. "I'll finish her," she mutters. June Spoon backs up. Jen starts chasing her around the dining room table waving the blade. I retreat to the lanai and watch through the sliding glass door. "Stop," June Spoon begs, "please, stop!" The chasing continues. Good thing June Spoon's wearing sneakers. "I'll give you the money, Jen!" My sister quits chasing. June Spoon lowers her head and leans against the hutch, trying to catch her breath. "I'm so so sorry," Jen says, rubbing June Spoon's back. They hug beside Madonna with Child.

COCONUT FOR BAIT

JUNE SPOON GETS MAD whenever Dadio swings at flies with rolled-up newspapers. Sometimes he swings at roaches. He doesn't seem to care that someone might still want to check out the news. I hate it when he uses the sports section. Dadio dislikes animals, insects, and most creatures of the sea. I know he despises his kids, especially me. He avoids petting dogs and cats. When he's not swatting flies, he busies himself fumigating the house with Had-A-Bug to kill mosquitoes and setting traps for rats in the attic. He uses coconut meat for bait. Believe it or not, he once caught a crimson cardinal. Don't ask me how that bird got in there, but he did. June Spoon told me that was Popsy's favorite bird. She cried for days. She even suggested the cardinal was the reincarnation of Popsy, and that God guided him to our home so he could listen to her soothing voice through the ceiling. She said Dadio might be guilty of murder, because reincarnation gave you a second chance at life before the Final Judgment. Dadio overhead June Spoon's accusation and smirked, mostly because he didn't believe in God or life-after-death or "that reincarnation hogwash."

The week of the bird murder, June Spoon fakes stomach flu to avoid sex after a bottle of Lancer's and *The Ed Sullivan Show*. Now she's going to sleep long after Dadio pulls on his pajamas. "Get to bed,

June," he scolds from their room on a windy night, his sullen voice rattling down the hall. June Spoon sits at the dining room table, reading a crumpled paper stained with fly guts. "In a minute, Dear," she lies. She bites into an Almond Mounds while perusing the Obits. She loves it how the women outlive the men, usually by a decade and sometimes even more. She's certain Dadio will return either as a fly or a mosquito, one that will bug her to no end all hours of the day and night. She prays for a fly. She imagines a big horse-fly buzzing a hunk of snow-white coconut perched on the table. Yesterday she bought a jumbo swatter at Longs Drugs, a pink one with a comfy handle she hid in her bathroom cabinet under the sink. She washes the Mounds down with tea. June Spoon smiles. She imagines swatting Dadio to end his second shot at life. She figures God won't accuse her of murder since she's merely avenging Popsy's death as a bird. "Eye for an eye," June Spoon whispers into the night.

NOTES FROM THE FRONT LINE

LIVER SPOTS erupt on Dadio's last postcard. Troy's busy lipsticking pigs across town—he dolls up foreclosures with faux granite counters, elongated toilets, and synthetic lawns. June Spoon and Jen go Churching, pray for our souls. The dude on Fry Hill maintains his persona guzzling suds and cussing his mutt.

Google Earth me, stare at my block from Mars. I'm under that tar and gravel roof on the corner. Yes, that's a doughboy pool out back. Underpants frozen on lines, stinking of bleach. The bird feeder's stuffed with black seeds: sparrows chirp iambic pentameter. A hobo tortoise claws through the weeds, searching for purpose.

THE ENEMY TREE

DADIO'S GOT a hobby. He paints a face on a coconut shell, ties dental floss to a furniture tack, and sinks the tack into the shell's crown. He dangles the face off a jacaranda out back. There must be fifty faces already hanging on that tree. Each represents an enemy. Some of the faces have Xed out eyes. Others look like demons. A few remind me of stooges. Who are these people? I know he hates Ross the neighbor. He also hates that Marine down the street with the RV. Sometimes he even hates June Spoon. I spot one on a lower branch with slits for eyes and a big mouth. "Who's that?" I ask, pointing. Dadio stares at me and smiles.

HORSE-FLIES

I DON'T KNOW how to say this, but Dadio's farting horse-flies. I'm not sure how that's possible, but here they come, one after another, wings filling the room.

"Is that the burrito talking?" I ask.

"Not sure," Dadio answers. He lifts his leg, farts blue, and out come two more.

I think it's a death sign. Dadio's finito and this is his last hurrah. I roll up the sports section and swing.

"Don't!" goes Dadio.

"Why the hell not?"

"They're my masterpiece," he answers, smiling as they wax their wings on the windows and dance on the lights.

BOOK 7

NOTHING EVER CHANGES

SON OF CRAB

I AM A SICK MAN lying on a twin bed listening to rain. I have learned cold showers in a solar house inhabited by crabs. Dadio crab sits in a wheelchair clicking his remote. June Spoon crab devours mahi-mahi out of a doggie bag. I have the maid's room. The maid left years ago. The crabs go to bed at midnight, him in his hospital bed with a view of the red ti garden, her in the king they once shared. They would claw one another when the salmon curtains were drawn. Now they scuttle through the house searching for water, entertainment, and dead things to eat. Outside, rain floods the street. My skin hardens as I write.

BIG BROTHER

FIRST LOVE was a raven-haired beauty that cheered for the boys who did what he dreamt of doing on football fields and parquet floors. Now Troy's 59. Unmarried. A *manju* who rents companionship by the month. Jamaican Jane just moved out of his Waikiki townhouse, says she refuses to 'work' for minimum.

Troy buys auctioned properties and refurbishes—Brazilian granite countertops, Asian blue quartz tile, elongated toilets. He makes a tidy profit. He combs the Internet for the next foreclosure before the hollow returns, the empty caused by the man who spied on his teenage tryouts and always told him he would never make the cut.

Troy cancels Dadio's hospice at Kahala Nui. He smuggles in pudding laced with Mexican penicillin and spoon-feeds behind closed doors. Dadio gags.

"You're torturing him," I tell Troy.

"How?" he asks.

"That pudding's falling into his lungs."

He continues spooning. "You just want Dadio dead."

"Why's that?"

"So you can get his money."

Dadio coughs, spits up a glob of chocolate.

note:

manju: tightwad

ASSISTED LIVING

DADIO'S IN BED wearing a Halloween mask. He's Br'er Rabbit. It's not Halloween or anything but he paid an orderly to pre-shop at the Pick 'n Save across the street. He wears the jumpsuit part of the costume like a bib and there's a scene of Br'er Rabbit munching a carrot in the Briar Patch. I spot a steak knife stuck in the ceiling, the end result of Dadio's fit last year on his birthday. I tell him my wife's expecting. He says nothing.

He tells me to get his wheelchair because he wants to trick-or-treat fellow patients. "It's not Halloween yet," I tell him. "So what," he grumbles. "They won't have treats." Dadio studies the knife. "Then they'll get tricks." I ask what kind of tricks he has in mind. He says he'll pull the plugs that keep them alive or maybe spill water on their machines so electricity shocks their spines. I don't know where he gets this stuff.

A nurse brings in a slice of carrot cake from a patient's birthday down the hall. He looks at it on his tray, his eyes milk glass blue through the holes in the mask. "Dadio?" He slaps the cake and it sails off his tray onto the carpet. "No more birthdays," he goes, "tomorrow the rabbit dies."

DADIO

BETWEEN ROOMS, a shadow hunches behind the rice paper panel. It's spying. There's the stink of lavender pomade. "Dadio?" I go. He whispers from the afterlife, tells me God doesn't exist. "Atheist," I scold. I know his voice will always be in me, the way his face haunts mirrors. He says there needs to be more of him in me, that I should try harder in life before I'm pushing the daisies. "Begone, Dadio," I mumble. "Suit yourself," he answers, slinking off to the washroom.

SOON YOUR EYES ADJUST

I STROLL A FIELD of lavender and wandering cows. I reach a fence of rectangular black boxes joined by wire. A priest hurdles the fence—he's swinging chains attached to a smoking gold thurible. The aroma of frankincense makes me think of Church. I pat a white cow's forehead. I realize the black boxes in the fence aren't boxes at all but upright coffins. I knock on one. The lid opens—Dadio pops out in a tuxedo. His hair's slicked back and he's got a good tan.

"You look great, Dadio," I say.

"It's dark at first," he goes, "but soon your eyes adjust."

"How's June Spoon?"

"She over here already?" he asks.

"Since last May," I tell him. "Any words of wisdom?"

He nods. "Whatever you do, son, don't hop this fence."

Dadio cartwheels through the lavender. The cows watch. Bees leave the blossoms and buzz the wisps of frankincense. The priest plops down his thurible. He saunters over and whispers in Dadio's ear.

Dadio frowns. He kicks the thurible like a football and it sails over the fence. He marches back into his coffin. The priest slams the lid shut.

AT FAT ALBERT'S, SELLWOOD

HAPPY BIRTHDAY, DADIO. I'm playing counter boy in memory of you at this greasy spoon. I squeak on my vinyl stool and toy with a paper napkin. I try folding it into an angel. You'd tell me to act my age. My counter mates? A model-thin blonde in a Reed College sweatshirt and a bald man thumbing *The Oregonian.* The stink of fried eggs makes me nauseous. The waitress slides over a menu— she's doubling as the cook. I contemplate specials as steam fogs my cup.

Moments of indecision always summon you. "Learn to be decisive," you barked. I was your thorn, a chronic pain infected by the disgust of never making you proud. "Worthless," you mumbled one New Year's Eve. I learned defeat in our closed-door sessions, when screams and *I'm-sorry-Daddy's* joined the beat of the belt. I touched my wall and felt sorrow moving in waves through the redwood.

I vow to quit remembering. Memories send me beyond blue, into the indigo sky before twilight. Dadio, you carried hate into the hospital bed, where I spoon-fed you vanilla pudding and rubbed your feet under the sheets. Cold feet, I thought, icy heart. A nurse checked your pulse. "No more flowers," you scolded when my Christmas anthuriums arrived. I swore you'd never die but, if you did, I'd lug you like an overstuffed suitcase into the future.

NOTHING EVER CHANGES

I'M OVER AT JEN'S fixing the toilet. That gasket between the tank and the bowl's leaking. Water everywhere. The tiles are soaked not only from the toilet but also from the shower. Jen has yet to replace the torn curtain.

My sister's big into spells. There's this guy in Munich she likes so she keeps a rose on a tarot card under her bed. The Lovers card. I think she's getting a bit old for this voodoo stuff, considering she's closing in on fifty. But what can I say? Every time she visits a psychic they tell what she wants to hear—that she'll be a fabulously wealthy movie star and the mother of twins. She hasn't had a date in years, although a schizoid from New Delhi claimed she slept with her husband. Who knows.

Jen spends her days searching for signs: ladybugs in her window, squirrels balancing on telephone lines, geese flying over her roof. Once she got giddy when a moth circled the light on her nightstand. "What's the big deal?" I asked. "An invitation from overseas," she said. "What kind of invitation?" I continued. She put her hands on her hips. "Something romantic," she answered. One thing about Jen, she sure casts a wide net with her vague prophecies. She claims we knew each other in another life, only I was her slave. "Nothing ever changes," I tell her, tightening the nut on her tank.

THE MUSEUM

DADIO KICKS the bucket. A month after the service, Troy uses the hallway to memorialize his heroics in the Big War. There are medals, pins and ribbon bars behind glass, dog tags, photos of Dadio aiming guns and posing in jeeps, and portraits documenting his rise from second lieutenant to major. Always a different hat. Never showing his teeth.

Troy flicks on the hallway light—a narrow corridor stretches from the kitchen to the bedrooms. The walls are redwood. I flash to a boy running on bloody legs as Dadio curses swinging a belt. Troy studies what's hanging. "Guess where I found that gold oak leaf," he goes. "In the old footlocker?" I ask. "On eBay," he gloats. I think all this staging is getting the best of my bro. I mean, that oak leaf belongs to another soldier.

I'm not sure who'll appreciate the museum. The Filipina cleaning lady hasn't said a word. Friends rarely drop by. June Spoon walks the hallway a dozen times a day but I doubt she even glances at the man stuffed in uniforms. She keeps the light off. The hallway stinks of mildew as her slippers churn dead roaches with the ghosts of children.

RECLUSE

JEN WANTS to hide out. "Hide out from what?" I ask. "Life," she answers. I'm not sure what brought this on, although I suspect it has something to do with Dadio beating us. He beat me mostly, but he beat her too because she had to live through my screams. She got so good at disappearing I figured she'd become the next David Copperfield. She's deadly serious about moving to either the German countryside or a remote island inhabited by flightless birds. She thinks it's brave to run, but I feel she's being a coward. I scare her when I say no husband and no children mean dying alone in Bavaria or in the middle of the Pacific. I mention the option of marriage, since it requires semi-seclusion behind walls and doors. "Make babies in the dark," I smile. "Ew, sick," she mutters, "I hate bald, gurgling creatures." She recoils imagining sharing a house with a man. "I suppose he expects me to cook," she groans. I suggest wedding a chef or someone who frequents the farmer's market. "Will he like pasta?" she asks. "Sure," I go, "most guys love Italian." She lightens up after I tell her he'll be busy working and she'll be by herself most of the day. I remind her that, if she does end up with a chef, he'll be at the restaurant all night and will snooze away the sunshine hours. "Rarely cross paths," I whisper. "I suppose you're right," she admits, "as long as this dude respects my privacy." She says she has a good recipe for salmon and may bake every two weeks, that is, if he doesn't expect her to answer the door and pretends she's a ghost holidays and weekends.

SWIMMING UPSTREAM

I WAKE CURSING Troy. I know it's abnormal. But my big brother's light years away from being a garden-variety sibling. His latest epic is a 13-page character assassination of yours truly, faulting me for everything under the sun, from swiping 1960s cassette recordings of Gramma talking story, to flunking out of law school, to pretending I was a bartender at Sea World. Wow, I like the idea of serving drinks to Shamu! Anyway, if we were back in the time of Jesus, my brother would be the first in the mob to pick up a stone. Troy's hardly a Saint. I never faulted him for tax evasion, identity theft, creating fictitious bank accounts, hiring prostitutes on a weekly basis, or having his underworld pals steal his Ranchero so he could collect insurance proceeds.

I think Troy's anger can be traced back to Dadio. He beat us at the slightest provocation: he cut me open with the metal buckle on his belt during a strapping, and Troy got whipped for drinking chocolate milk without permission. Dadio's rage somehow transferred to Troy, to the degree my brother seems ten times worse than his creator. His hobby is talking stink about everyone. Now he's brainwashing June Spoon, June Spoon. She believes everything he says about me, including accusations of being a coke fiend, stealing family photo albums (I must admit I lifted a picture of Gramma on horseback), and that I must hate her since I rarely visit. I'm pretty sure he's convinced June Spoon to remove my name as beneficiary on her life insurance policy. Next I'll be accused of grand larceny or even murder. I suppose it really doesn't matter, not in the long run. My words will outlive June Spoon, Troy, and even me. Someday someone, maybe you, will read my story as a storm builds, thunder rumbles, and rain streams over our graves.

UNDER THE STRUDEL ROOF

JEN IS A MILLION MILES away in Bavaria nursing her father figure complex. She lives in snow with Wolfgang, a widower who drives a vintage BMW to Lion's Club meetings in Munich and Kempten. Jen is playing the cool Euro Babe but she's really hiding out while trying to force a marriage. She's always felt bad never finding Mister Right while all her girlhood pals got married and had children. My sister aches for Wolfgang's proposal. He must realize Jen is trying to buy love after she buttered him up with a roundtrip ticket to Boston and a weeklong stay at a swanky Old Harbor hotel. I realized there was something wrong after she made June Spoon cough up $500 for a love spell. Lordy. Then, as if to seal the deal, she slipped The Lovers tarot card under her mattress. She pays her German $1,000/month for a room that once served as a nursery. If they were intimate, wouldn't Jen be sharing his room? In pictures, Wolfgang seems uneasy as she leans toward him trying to make contact. It's strange seeing a 40-something blonde posing with what looks like Andy Warhol's father. I know he's counting on her as both a nurse and a purse in his twilight years. Wolfgang has to be Dark Ages ancient because he loves Elvis, especially "Don't Be Cruel" and "Fool's Fall in Love." I wonder what he thinks when Jen rocks out to her bands from the Eighties, such as The Cure, Depeche

Mode, and David Bowie.

My sister brags about cooking goose with squash in a gas oven. Her goal is to make apple strudel, Wolfgang's holiday favorite. She imagines a big Munich wedding and a reception filled with international guests speaking every language under the sun. Next comes a Hawaiian honeymoon, followed by a baby giggling on a bearskin rug. Maybe, back at SDSU, Jen should have birthed that Iggy Pop look-alike's child instead of having me drive to the clinic. Now I think her biological clock's kaput. But I can't tell Jen anything because she's a Taurus and bull-headed. She believes dressing young keeps her body young, as if her eggs will always be fresh if she wears stiletto-heeled boots, mini-skirts, and fishnet stockings.

I'm not allowed to speak to Wolfgang. Jen thinks I might spit some truth she's slaved months to hide. She made me and June Spoon swear to never reveal her age. It's verboten to visit. All I can do is send cheerful holiday cards and call her cell on birthdays. The phone number to the house is a secret.

At dawn I check Munich's weather. I subtract five degrees because Jen lives close to the Alps. Sometimes I use Google Earth to find Wolfgang's home on a country road. I max zoom—the roof has a slight pitch and its rectangular tiles are dusted white. The tiles remind me of strudel. I picture my sister under this strudel roof. She is cooking to please an old man, as snow the texture of powdered sugar sprinkles the township of Weitnau-Rechtis.

REUNION WITH A LOST FRIEND

We meet at the pub's fire pit. I'm the impoverished writer and you're the big bucks surgeon. I have a wife and you do too. We order brews. Our women celebrate with Champagne. Who picks up the tab? Now your hair and beard are silver. We flirt with the Dublin waitress as if we're both still freshmen and our wives are really our mothers. A half-life has passed since we redlined the Trans Am and blew up before Winnemucca. Remember the Red Bull Casino and trying to change our luck?

You tell football stories that I know aren't true, such as catching a touchdown pass as a guard. I nod, pretending your memories are real. I imagine you doing a sideline pattern and snatching the brown orb in the corner of the end zone. We were both guards, blocking for an eggshell quarterback who feigned concussions and ran like a girl.

We eat beef and our women eat chicken. Our better halves gossip about Oregon. I order a second brew and you do too. I thank you for letting me hide in your dorm room the night the cops were hunting me down. Face it, you were my shadow in college. You hated Laura after she snuck in through my window—don't think I didn't recognize your red knock at the door. To make up, I drove you twenty miles off-campus to visit your hippie chick with the infant daughter. Your weakness was always older women.

Our waitress sticks the vinyl check presenter in front of you. The band inside plays hillbilly music. An awkward silence turns your blue eyes to ash. Finally, you pluck out the bill and study it. You wince paying with Visa and demand half in cash, including the tip. We hug outside the pub. Our wives hug too and vow to stay in touch. I watch you stroll the gas lamp boardwalk through halos of light, until you and your woman vanish.

ABOUT THE AUTHOR

Kirby Wright was born and raised in Honolulu, Hawaii. He is a graduate of Punahou School in Honolulu and the University of California at San Diego. He received his MFA in Creative Writing from San Francisco State University. Wright has been nominated for four Pushcart Prizes and is a past recipient of the *Honolulu Weekly* Nonfiction Prize, the *Honolulu Weekly* Poetry Prize, the Jodi Stutz Memorial Prize in Poetry, the Ann Fields Poetry Prize, the Academy of American Poets Award, the Robert Browning Award for Dramatic Monologue, and Arts Council Silicon Valley Fellowships in Poetry and The Novel. Before the City, his first poetry collection, took First Place at the 2003 San Diego Book Awards. Wright is also the author of the companion novels *Punahou Blues* and *Moloka'i Nui Ahina*, both set in Hawaii. He was a Visiting Fellow at the 2009 International Writers Conference in Hong Kong, where he represented the Pacific Rim region of Hawaii. He was also a Visiting Writer at the 2010 Martha's Vineyard Residency in Edgartown, Mass. and the 2011 Artist in Residence at Milkwood International, Czech Republic. *The End, My Friend*, his futuristic thriller, was released in 2013.

LEMON SHARK PRESS

—FALL 2013 BOOK LAUNCH—
San Diego writer Kirby Wright will introduce
His Futuristic Thriller
THE END MY FRIEND: Prelude to the Apocalypse.

*UPSTART CROW BOOKSTORE & COFFEEHOUSE
*835C West Harbor Drive, Seaport Village
*San Diego, 92101
*Friday, September 27th, 2013
*7 pm—9 pm
*Local Musician Bill Ostrie on Guitar

Contact: lemonsharkpress@yahoo.com

LEMON SHARK PRESS

—OKTOBERFEST BOOKS, BREW & MUSIC—

Celebrate Oktoberfest in style with IRON FIST BREWING CO. & Vista writer Kirby Wright. Kirby will be signing copies of his new Futuristic Thriller @ the Brewery.

*IRON FIST BREWING CO.
*1305 Hot Springs Way, Vista, 92081
*Saturday, October 19th, 2013
*noon—3 pm
*Local Musician Bill Ostrie on Guitar
*Must be 21+

Contact: lemonsharkpress@yahoo.com

www.ingramcontent.com/pod-product-compliance
Lightning Source LLC
Chambersburg PA
CBHW021920170626
46807CB00007B/2912